CHICANO, AMIGO

MAURINE H. GEE

CHICANO, AMIGO

ILLUSTRATED BY TED LEWIN

1972
WILLIAM MORROW AND COMPANY NEW YORK

Printed in the United States of America.
Library of Congress Catalog Card Number 70-174578
1 2 3 4 5 76 75 74 73 72

By the Same Author

FIRESTORM

FLOOD HAZARD

CONTENTS

MARC'S CHICANO

There are days in Southern California when the January sun bears down as hot as though it were midsummer. Marc Conley was sweating as he and Gonny Gonzales left the school grounds on their bikes headed for Mr. Brenner's house. Mr. Brenner was cubmaster of Pack 103.

"I still don't like the idea of trying to teach a bunch of cub scouts magic tricks," Gonny grumbled. "They think they know everything already."

Gonny was eleven, a month younger than Marc, who was tickled to see him getting cold feet about facing a bunch of eight-year-olds.

"You only have them this one day," he said. "I have to think up games and stuff for them every week."

"Hey, watch it!" Gonny yelled.

His warning was too late. A little kid burst out of the shrubbery off to the right and dashed in front of Marc. Marc swerved sharply, but the collision threw the boy back against the curbing and upset Marc's bicycle. He picked himself up and looked around.

Husky Erv Tatum, the bully of Den 3, had jumped on the fallen runner and was trying to pound the stuffing out of him. The victim was Kiki, a young boy who wanted to join the cub scouts of Den 3. He hung around outside Mr. Brenner's house every time Den 3 was having its Friday meeting, listening at the door or peeking in the window.

Somewhere he had got hold of a battered wolf cub-scout book. Then, one day when Marc was wearing his scout uniform, Kiki had cornered him and rattled off the cub-scout promise. He gave the wrong answers to the other four things that a cub has to do to earn his bobcat badge, but afterward he seemed to figure that someone owed him something. He was a pest, but Marc couldn't stand there and let Erv beat on him.

Marc caught Erv by the shoulder and tried to pull him off the little kid.

"He's got to stop bugging me," Erv panted. "Every time I wear my uniform he hangs around."

"You can't beat up on him just for that," Marc protested.

Erv didn't agree. He ducked lower and went right on with his pounding. Marc grabbed a fistful of Erv's molasses-colored hair and hauled him to his feet. Erv howled his protest and began kicking Marc.

Marc got hotter than ever around his neatly folded neckerchief. When Erv wouldn't stop, Marc folded him over the seat of the fallen bike and gave him a paddling.

Other kids gathered around shouting advice and encouragement. "Atta boy, Marc, dust off his britches," urged a shrill voice.

"Give him one for me," sang out another.

"If your hand wears out, I got one here you can borrow."

Finally Marc turned Erv loose. He scrambled to his feet, clutching the seat of his pants as though he were on fire. Still, he pointed to Kiki, who had paused in his flight to watch the fascinating spectacle of Erv Tatum getting a proper licking. "I'm not going to let Marc's stinking Chicano join our den. Not now or ever."

"Yeah, Marc's Chicano," mocked one of the hecklers.

Marc picked up his bike and waved Erv on his way. When Erv had moved off to a safe distance, he yelled at Marc, "Wait till my big brother hears about this. He'll get you. You'll get what's coming to you."

"Sure, bring him along," Gonny answered for Marc. "We're looking for a gringo like you who doesn't have such a big mouth." He rode on over beside Marc. "Come on, we'll be late for the meeting."

At that moment Marc noticed the bloody gash on Kiki's knee. "Look he's limping and bleeding all over the place," he said. "I'll give him a ride home."

"Forget it," Gonny urged. "He lives away over by the dump."

Marc rode off and overtook Kiki. The little guy

turned to him with a big grin. Tearstains showed on his cheeks, but his smile was something to see.

"You did fine," he told Marc. "I bet the next time Erv jumps me he's going to be sure you're not around."

"Come on, I'll give you a lift home," Marc said. "You've got to get a bandage on that knee."

Kiki yanked up a handful of long grass from beside the path and started wiping away the blood.

"Not that way," protested Marc. "You've got to clean it with alcohol or soap and water. Then you put on a clean bandage to keep out the dirt."

Kiki chuckled. "Aw, I don't worry about the knee," he said, settling himself on the crossbar of Marc's bicycle. "I just don' want to get blood on the bicycle."

Marc looked back over his shoulder and saw that Gonny was following them slowly, keeping his distance. When he saw Marc looking his way, he held his nose with one hand and made an urgent gesture with the other to indicate that Marc was headed in the wrong direction. Marc paid no attention.

"Maybe we get a little bad smell from the dump,"

Kiki said, as he directed Marc to a small frame house, which stood off by itself on a plot of filled land. It once had been a real-estate office, and half the sign still was attached to the roof. "Before we move here, we live in one room with another family to share the kitchen and the bathroom. Here is wonderful with everything just for us."

The little house was perched on cement blocks as though it were prepared to take off at a moment's

notice. A battered blue sedan without wheels stood in the front yard, and three little kids were hopping in and out of it, yelling and laughing as they played. A woman with long black hair was going around the yard with a bucket, flicking out handfuls of water to quiet down the dust.

At the sight of Marc and Kiki the little kids let out shrieks of welcome, but the woman retreated hastily to the house and called them inside.

"My *mamá* speaks no English," said Kiki. "She is timid with the strangers. Come inside, and I will show you my fine slingshot with which I kill the gophers."

"Some other time," said Marc.

"It would be an honor for my *mamá* to meet the big shot of the cub scouts," Kiki said.

"I'm only the den chief," said Marc. "Mr. Brenner is the boss."

"Hey, come on," Gonny shouted from the road.

Good old Gonny. "I've got to get on to the meeting," Marc said. Although he felt that he ought to see that Kiki cleaned the cut knee properly before it was bandaged, he didn't like the idea of meeting the woman and all those giggly kids. "You can show me the slingshot later," he promised.

Gonny was a good friend, but there were times when Marc couldn't figure him out at all. "I don't get it," he said, as they rode along toward Mr. Brenner's. "You're Mexican-American same as Kiki and yet you treat him like dirt."

"You're not supposed to understand," said Gonny, not at all concerned. "You don't know what a struggle my mother and my father had to get where they are. My dad's the best veterinarian in our part of the valley, and we're the only Mexican-Americans in our neighborhood. How long would we be welcome if we had Kiki and his kind hanging around?"

"It wouldn't hurt you," said Marc.

Gonny shook his head. "You'll get your snoot full of your little Chicano before this is over. You'll wish you had let Erv teach him a thing or two."

"He's not my Chicano," Marc protested.

"You want to bet?" Gonny challenged.

Marc let the question go. They had reached Mr. Brenner's house, and he had important chores on his mind.

TARGET ONE

Friday, after school, Gonny handed Marc a note that was tightly sealed.

"Where'd you get this?" Marc asked, thinking it must be some kind of a joke.

Gonny shrugged. "A little kid said it was for you. I've seen him around."

Marc read the note. "You beat up my brother for the last time. I'm going to get you. Not on the school grounds. I will catch you someplace else and knock your teeth down your throat. I will also jump on the wheels of your bike and wreck every spoke. You know who."

"Sounds like Roy Tatum," said Marc. "Erv's been working on him."

He handed the note to Gonny. Gonny's brows shot up as he read the message. "What you going to do about it?" he asked.

"How do I know?" Marc protested. "I've got to think about it. I won't see him till Monday, so that gives me plenty of time to work out something."

"Don't yell at me," said Gonny. "No one's pushing you. It's just that Roy is such a big slob. I'd sure hate to have him laying for me."

"So would I," said Marc shortly, as he stuffed the note in his pocket. "Now let's forget him for five minutes."

Gonny nodded. "Suits me," he agreed.

"And keep it to yourself," Marc urged. "I don't want the other kids making wisecracks. They'd like to blow this up to a big fight."

"I won't say a word," Gonny promised. "Just stop yelling at me, that's all. I didn't write the note."

Still, Roy's threats continued to haunt Marc, and when Monday rolled around he decided not to ride his bicycle to school. Gonny idled along beside him, with Marc's books in the carton on his bicycle.

"Maybe I should read that note again," Gonny said. "Maybe Roy was just kidding."

"He was not kidding," said Marc. "He means business."

"What did your dad say about it?" Gonny asked

"I didn't say anything to him," Marc admitted. "I decided Roy is my problem. He'd laugh if I hid behind my dad or mother, like having her drive me to school and then pick me up."

Gonny eyed him shyly. "But you thought about it," he said.

"Sure," Marc admitted.

"You plan to fight Roy?" Gonny asked, a glimmer of anticipation in his eyes. "He sure thinks he's the toughest kid in school."

Marc shook his head. "I just got the braces off my teeth," he reminded Gonny. "I don't plan to take on more braces and rubber bands."

"Too bad that Erv isn't an only child," said Gonny.

"I've been trying to figure it out," said Marc. "Maybe I should take it up with my counselor at school. He would call the three of us to his office and squash the whole thing."

"Why don't you tell Roy that Erv jumped on a kid half his size?" Gonny asked.

"Because I don't have a loudspeaker, that's why," said Marc. "I'm staying clear of that guy till he cools off."

Gonny sighed. "You've got a problem."

When they reached the school grounds, they found an impatient Kiki waiting for them. He beamed at Marc, his eyes shining with trust and admiration.

"Don't worry about the fight," he said breathlessly. "It's all my fault. I take care of everything."

Marc eyed him cooly. "What fight?" he asked.

"With Roy Tatum," said Kiki.

"Who says so?" Marc demanded.

"Erv has a big mouth," said Kiki. "But don' you worry. This time I am prepared."

"You stay out of this," Marc ordered. "I mean it."

"I hear you," said Kiki, and he gave Marc a foxy wink before he ran off.

Gonny sprawled on his bicycle and brushed his hands together, as though ridding them of dirt. "So much for deep secrecy," he said. "With that Kiki on your side, who's afraid of Roy?"

"Very funny," said Marc.

At three o'clock when Marc and Gonny left school, there were three other boys with them. On the way home, each of the others turned off at his own cross street until Marc and Gonny were on their own.

Soon the sidewalk gave way to a path that ran beside the embankment of Hidden Canyon Creek, which carried a mere trickle of water. Gonny circled around on his bicycle, keeping a sharp eye on the far side of bushes and tree trunks.

"Guess Roy got cold feet when he saw us take off with those other kids," he said. "Looks like your teeth are safe for another day."

"Suits me," said Marc.

Gonny made a wider sweep and came pumping back as though he would welcome a set of wings. "Roy's hiding out near the culvert," he reported.

Roy, looking as bulky and tough as a bull moose,

came up the embankment followed at a distance by brother Erv. Standing at the side of the path, Roy waited for Marc to come along. Marc did his best to keep up his brisk pace, and Gonny dropped back to see what would happen.

Roy stepped out on the path and blocked Marc's way. "Where's your bike?" he asked with a toothy smile. "How can I take care of your bike if you hide it out?"

"I'm not hiding anything," said Marc, his throat dry.

"Guess you got my message," Roy said. "Guess you know what to expect."

"I don't expect anything," said Marc. "I haven't done anything to you."

"It's my kid brother got hurt," said Roy. He kept his cold gray eyes on Marc, as he shook off his leather jacket and handed it to Erv. Erv made no effort to hide the smirk on his face.

"Look, Erv was picking on a kid half his size," said Marc earnestly. "Sure, I paddled him, but he had it coming."

Erv made a jeering noise. "Listen to him lie. He knows what's coming. He knows he's going to get a beating."

Marc's hands tightened into fists. "Here it comes," he told himself. He heard pounding footsteps on the path back of him, but he was too intent on Roy's big fists to pay much attention.

"Hold it!" sang out a shrill, breathless voice.

Marc looked over his shoulder, and there, on the stump of a sycamore, stood Kiki. He held a sturdy slingshot up before his face, all ready for action.

"Erv," Kiki called, "tell Roy you kept kicking Marc in the shins till he had to stop you. Tell him how you jumped me."

Roy's eyes wavered. "Get him, Erv," he yelled.

Erv dropped the leather jacket. Kiki drew back on the slingshot and let go. Erv staggered back and sat down very hard.

"I'm shot," he howled, clutching at his chest.

"Watch it, Roy," Kiki warned. "I got a bigger, smoother rock for you. All winter I shoot the gophers in the head. Your head makes a more big target."

Roy stood undecided, but Erv picked himself up and took off for home, bellowing with rage.

"Don' forget the story about David and Goliath," Kiki called to Roy. "Is true story. Can happen again."

Roy muttered to himself as he caught up his jacket and turned his back on the little guy with the slingshot. He took off after Erv in a long easy lope.

Marc took a deep breath. He was surprised to find that he was shaking all over. "Your bluff worked," he told Kiki.

Kiki got down off his perch. He limped as he came over to show Marc the smooth brown stone that he had aimed at Roy. "Is no bluff," he said. "For you, I knock him cold."

Boy, was he ever cocky Marc thought. "I hope Mr. Brenner doesn't hear about this," he said. "He won't let the cubs carry slingshots."

Kiki grinned. "I will repent," he promised. "I put away the slingshot and use it only on the gophers."

"Good," said Marc. "And thanks." He turned to Gonny. "How about giving Kiki a ride home?"

"Yeah, I noticed he was limping," said Gonny,

looking embarrassed. "Come on, kid. I just happen to be going past your place."

Kiki accepted the ride with dignity. "A good idea," he agreed. "I got to study up on the law of the pack and the cub-scout motto before I have my meeting with Mr. Brenner."

He raised his slingshot high in a salute to Marc as he rode off with Gonny.

HAPPY DAY

Wednesday afternoon Marc was out by the garage playing tip-in basketball with Gonny when he heard a persistent screechy sound. He glanced up in the eucalyptus trees, thinking it was a fussy bird scolding about something. But as the noise came closer, he saw skinny little Kiki toiling up the hill, pulling a rickety metal wagon, which once had been red.

Gonny groaned. "Here comes the giant killer," he said. "Here comes trouble."

"I seem to remember him," said Marc. "Why doesn't he put some grease on that squeaky wheel?"

"If he had any grease, he'd eat it," said Gonny. "How can he eat so much and stay so skinny?"

Kiki stopped the wagon and put a rock back of one wheel to keep it from coasting down the hill. Gonny ignored him while Marc bounced the ball and tried for the hoop. He missed. Kiki made him nervous standing there, so eager to speak up.

"Oye, amigo," Kiki called cautiously, as though he could not hold in the glad tidings another moment. "I did like you say. I went to Mr. Brenner and told him all that is in my heart, and he say I get to join Den 3 as soon as I get my uniform."

"That's great," said Marc.

"So now I collect soda-pop bottles and aluminum cans to make the money," said Kiki. "You think maybe you got some for me?"

"I don't know," said Marc. "But, at least, I've got some oil for that squeaky wheel."

Kiki beamed. He pointed to the neat bandage on his knee. "The school nurse fixed me up," he said. "Everybody help Kiki."

Gonny nudged Marc. “I hope you get the message,” he said. “How about cutting down your old uniform to fit the kid?”

“I gave it away long ago,” said Marc. “Come on, Kiki. Let’s oil up your wagon.”

He entered the garage by the side door and got the oil can from the workbench. Then he squirted the wobbly, dished-in wheels with oil and tightened the axle nuts.

“It’s for the uniform I need the money,” Kiki explained hurriedly. "When I get you for the friend, I say to myself, 'Why you don' get busy? Why you don' go on the camp-out with your friends?' So then I talk to Mr. Brenner, and he say the registration can wait, but I got to have the uniform before I can go along with you."

He was still puffing hard from dragging that wagon up the hill. It held an old tire, a dented five-gallon can, and a rusty grill, which had come from someone's barbecue pit. His black hair glistened with sweat, and pale rivulets streaked his cheeks.

"Mr. Brenner is a great guy," said Marc. "He's tops on a camp-out."

Kiki couldn't suppress a shiver of excited anticipation. "I worry for fear they sell my uniform at the Salvation Army store," he confided. "It is a guaranteed regulation uniform."

"How much is it?" Marc asked.

"Ninety-three cents," said Kiki. "Is too big, but soon I grow to fit him. When I join Den 3, I earn the merit badges fast to cover the dark spots on the shirt where the other scout had his badges."

"Sorry you hit me too late for my old uniform,"

said Marc. "I may still have the cap and scarf around somewhere."

Kiki drew in a short delighted breath. "Ah, look good," he begged. "My friend, Frederico, promises to take me to the Friday meeting if I get the uniform. Without the uniform, there is no hope."

Marc called to Gonny. "Help Kiki look in the trash barrels for cans and bottles," he urged. "I've got to look for my cub-scout cap and neckerchief."

He found the yellow scarf and the faded blue cap without too much trouble. As he went out through the kitchen, he paused at the cooky jar and took out a few for Kiki. The kid could use a little meat on his bones. Marc doubted that Kiki was more than four feet tall, and certainly he didn't weigh more than sixty pounds. A real skinny guy.

When Kiki started off down the hill, his face was alight with happiness. He was richer by a cap, a scarf, eight soft-drink bottles, four aluminum beer cans, and a stack of nut wafers.

"As long as you're here," Gonny called to him, "why don't you go on up the hill and see if Mr. Zamora has something stashed away?"

Kiki turned back. "Who is Mr. Zamora?" he asked.

"An old guy, caretaker of the house on the hill," said Gonny. "A Chicano."

Kiki thanked Gonny and headed his wagon up the hill. The wheels still squeaked, but not as loudly as before.

"Be sure to close that big iron gate after you," Marc called to him. "Mr. Zamora gets sore if it's left open."

Marc and Gonny returned to their game of tip-in. Suddenly the sound of screams mixed with the barking of dogs wafted down the canyon. Kiki was doing the screaming, and Mr. Zamora's dogs, Tarzan, the Great Dane, and Butch, the black-and-white Boston terrier, were doing the barking. Marc started up the road at a run.

"Aw, they won't hurt him," Gonny yelled.

Kiki came tearing down the road, his eyes wild with fright. Close on his heels loped fawn-colored Tarzan, with Butch racing to get ahead of him. Marc tried to brace himself, but the three hit him so hard they knocked him over backward. The dogs licked his face and frisked around in an effort to show how happy they were to see him again.

"Hey, get them off me," Marc yelled to Gonny.

Gonny was laughing so hard that he wasn't much help. Finally he got Tarzan by his choke collar and dragged him away. Marc scrambled to his feet and grabbed Butch. The little dog was snapping at Tarzan in jealous rage, sure that the big dog was getting more than his share of attention.

"We've got to get the dogs back inside the gate," said Marc. "Mr. Zamora will have a fit if they get lost."

He started up the hill calling to the dogs, but they were enjoying their freedom too much to pay any attention. They ran off to sniff around the roots of the eucalyptus trees that grew by the garage.

"Haven't you got a soup bone or something we can use to lure them up the hill?" Gonny asked.

But Marc had a better idea. He hurried to his back porch and got an old tennis ball. He held it out temptingly to Tarzan, then threw it as far as he could up the hill. Tarzan dashed after the ball, and as usual Butch tried to beat him to the catch. Marc raced after them. Tarzan came prancing back with the ball in his slobbery mouth and his head high to keep the

ball out of Butch's reach. The little dog leaped high, over and over again, getting more frantic every moment.

"See if you can find another ball on the back porch," Marc called to Gonny. "We need a ball for each dog, or we're going to end up with a dogfight on our hands."

Gonny never did show up with another ball, but Marc managed to get the dogs back inside the big double gate. Kiki's wagon was right there, just inside the gate, where it had been abandoned when the dogs came charging to greet him.

He looked sheepishly at Marc. "I think maybe best you take me to see Mr. Zamora," he said.

Marc sighed. "You never give up, do you?" he said.

Kiki gave that big shining grin of his. "It's all I got going for me," he said.

Marc closed the big gate and started on up the driveway, followed by Kiki and the dogs. He certainly hoped this story didn't get around at school. He was getting a little tired of hearing so much about Marc's Chicano. But he could not discuss the problem with Gonny, who was just looking for an excuse to say, "I told you so."

Long ago the front part of the white stucco house, where Mr. Zamora lived, had been destroyed by an earthquake. Any boy who lived in California knew that the state lay in a ring of fire, a region of volcanos and earthquakes that reached as far south as New Zealand, went through Japan, then crossed the Aleutians, and ran down the west coast of Central America and South America. The area was formed by the action of the floor of the Pacific Ocean nudging at the land masses that surround it. All very simple indeed.

Scientists always were saying that another major quake was long overdue in California, but Marc kept his fingers crossed and hoped that he never would be near the center of one. Hearing about distant ones was bad enough.

Great mounds of scarlet bougainvillaea hid the scars of the earthquake on the big house and trailed over on the tiled roof of the dovecote, which graced the guest quarters on the far side of the driveway. The property belonged to an estate, and no one could decide what to do with it. In the meantime, Mr. Zamora got paid to keep an eye on the place.

Marc found the old gentleman out in his vegetable garden, doing a little irrigating. He greeted Marc and eyed Kiki with interest.

"Who have we here?" he asked.

Kiki's confidence was restored at once. "Jose Francisco Moreno, at your service," he said, extending his hand politely. "You may call me Kiki."

Mr. Zamora answered in Spanish, and from that moment on Marc was an outsider.

"I have to get back to the house," he told them.

They broke off the hand gestures and the Spanish long enough to say they would see him later. Marc jogged down the driveway, happy to be rid of Kiki and his problems.

Marc and Gonny were still thumping away with the basketball when Mr. Zamora drove his battered pickup truck down the hill. He paused at the driveway a moment.

"This is the happiest day of my life," sang out Kiki, who sat beside him. "My friend, Mr. Zamora, give me and the wagon a ride home, and each Saturday he pays me to pull weeds from his garden. Now I get to pick up the uniform. Also I get to go on the camp-out."

"That's great," said Marc, who would be going on the camp-out too.

"Great," agreed Gonny, who had not the slightest intention of going on the camp-out. "Best news yet."

As Mr. Zamora drove on down the hill, Marc turned on Gonny fiercely. "Don't say a word," he ordered. "Not one word."

Gonny's eyes widened in hurt surprise. "Who's talking?" he asked.

Marc slammed the ball to him. "Play ball," he said. "And keep your thoughts to yourself."

BUTCH PRESSES HIS LUCK

The following Saturday morning Mrs. Conley called Marc to the kitchen, where the savory smell of vanilla and chocolate and fresh baking filled the air.

"Marc, have you done anything to annoy Mr. Zamora?" his mother asked.

Marc thought for a moment. "Not that I know of," he said. "Why?"

"He used to stop by with little gifts from his

garden," said Mrs. Conley. "But I haven't seen him lately."

"Kiki spends half his time up there now," said Marc. "His family probably gets all the fresh vegetables."

His mother handed him a light package wrapped in foil. "Take this cake up the hill to Mr. Zamora. Tell him I've been worried about him."

"Um, sure smells good," Marc hinted.

"Don't peek," warned Mrs. Conley. "You'll spoil the frosting. There'll be a piece here for you when you get back."

Marc decided to walk. Getting his bike out for that short haul wasn't worth the trouble. He found the front gate closed, as usual, but there was something missing. He couldn't figure out what it was until he was halfway up the driveway and realized that Tarzan and Butch had not come running to meet him.

When he got nearer the house, he saw that Mr. Zamora's pickup was gone, and Kiki was out near the big oak, playing with the dogs. He was yelling instructions to them, as he threw an abused tennis ball for them to chase. The game was good exercise for the dogs, but presented the usual problem. Tarzan always caught the ball on the first bounce which left Butch snapping and lunging at the big dog. Even now he was all foamy at the mouth from yapping, and he was getting more frantic every moment.

"What are the dogs doing out?" Marc called to Kiki. "Mr. Zamora always shuts them up when he leaves the place."

"I take pity on them," said Kiki, a dramatic undertone to his voice. "I cannot bear to hear them beg to get out."

"So go put them right back again," said Marc.

Kiki couldn't believe anyone would be so cruel. "How would you like to be shut up in a dark place on such a fine day?" he asked.

"Don't give me that stuff," protested Marc. "Put them back where they were."

"Just one more little throw," said Kiki. "That Butch is so pushy he tickles me."

Marc went on into the kitchen to put the cake in the refrigerator. Suddenly Butch's yelps of rage were drowned out by an anguished howl from the deep-

voiced Tarzan. Marc reached the back door in time to see Butch's strong jaws clamped shut on Tarzan's throat. There he hung, his sturdy body swinging back and forth as Tarzan tried to shake him off. The big dog's fawn-colored throat was smeared with blood.

Kiki stood there yelling, "Marc! Come quick!"

Before Marc could reach them, Tarzan threw Butch clear. The hate-crazed little terrier rolled over a couple of times, then sprang to his feet and rushed back at Tarzan. The Great Dane seemed to figure that he had taken enough. He grabbed Butch by the nape of his neck and shook him savagely. Marc seized

Tarzan's choke collar, but he might as well have been trying to choke the trunk of a tree. At last he caught up a flower stake, thrust it under the chain, and twisted it until Tarzan gasped for breath. Butch fell free and lay motionless on the ground, a broken soggy heap.

Marc released Tarzan and warned him away. The big dog slunk off as though he were truly ashamed of himself.

Kiki was crying as he bent over Butch. "I killed him," he wailed. "I killed him."

Marc turned on him fierecely. "He's not dead," he shouted. "He's still breathing. We've got to get him to Doc Gonzales."

He ran into the house and caught up a shaggy bath mat off the service porch. Then he ran back to Butch and eased him gently onto the mat. Butch was putting up a different kind of fight now. He was fighting for every breath as Marc lifted him in his arms.

Kiki kept getting in the way. "I'm sorry, I'm sorry," he was saying. "I try to teach the dogs to be friends."

Marc wanted to kick him. "I'll take Butch down home and get mother to drive us to the vet's," he said.

"Me, too," said Kiki.

"No," said Marc. "You stay here, and when Mr. Zamora gets back, tell him I had to take Butch to Doc Gonzales."

Kiki returned to his wailing. "I can't tell him," he protested. "He'll kill me."

Marc paid no attention. He cradled Butch in his arms and hurried down the hill. Blood seeped through the mat and trickled down his arms. Even before he got home, he could see that the garage door was open and the car was gone. His mother probably had gone off on some errand.

Now what? he thought.

He would have to ride his bicycle to the vet's, but how was he going to carry Butch? Tenderly he placed the dog in a shady spot on the grass, while he got a length of rope and a big paper carton from the garage. Hurriedly he punched four holes in the box, tied it to the rack of his bicycle, and then placed Butch in it. Butch now was out cold, and he lay quietly in the box, breathing hard, as Marc took him down the canyon road headed for Doctor Gonzales's Dog and Cat Hospital.

Marc kept hoping that he would meet his mother's

car or Mr. Zamora's pickup before he got to the foot of the hill. But he had no such good luck. He was bushed and the bath mat was soggy with blood by the time he made it to the doctor's office. Doctor Gonzales himself took the little dog from Marc's arms.

"Hm," he said. "The Zamora dog. He's a scrapper, no mistake about that. I suppose he tried to finish off that Great Dane again."

"Yes, sir," said Marc, wiping his arm across his sweaty forehead. "Will he be all right?"

"He's a rough little fellow," said Doctor Gonzales, as he carried Butch into the glistening-white operating room. "You can be sure we'll do our best for him."

The doctor's assistant came in and eased Marc out to the waiting room. He knew Butch was in good hands, but he couldn't bear to go off and leave him. Sinking down in the nearest chair, he sat there, sweating.

It seemed to him that he waited there for hours. When he could stand the strain no longer, he opened the inside door an inch or two. He caught a glimpse of Butch, stretched out on the white table, quiet as could be, with patches of purple-colored antiseptic all over him.

Marc felt a hand on his shoulder, turned, and faced Mr. Zamora, with Kiki lagging behind him.

"It wasn't Tarzan's fault," Marc blurted out. "Butch jumped him."

"Kiki told me," said Mr. Zamora softly. "He says he will repent."

Marc gulped. He wanted to say a few things about that little stinker, but Mr. Zamora's hand squeezed his shoulder. "It's all right." he said. "He's learned a lesson."

Marc nodded. "I guess that Butch has learned a lesson, too." he said. "He'll think twice before he jumps Tarzan again."

"Butch learns nothing," said Mr. Zamora with a sigh. "If I didn't watch him like a hawk, he'd spend all his time here with Doctor Gonzales. They keep me broke."

Doctor Gonzales came to the door, wiping his hands on a fresh towel. He smiled a greeting to Mr. Zamora. "Well," he said, "your prizefighter had a close call.

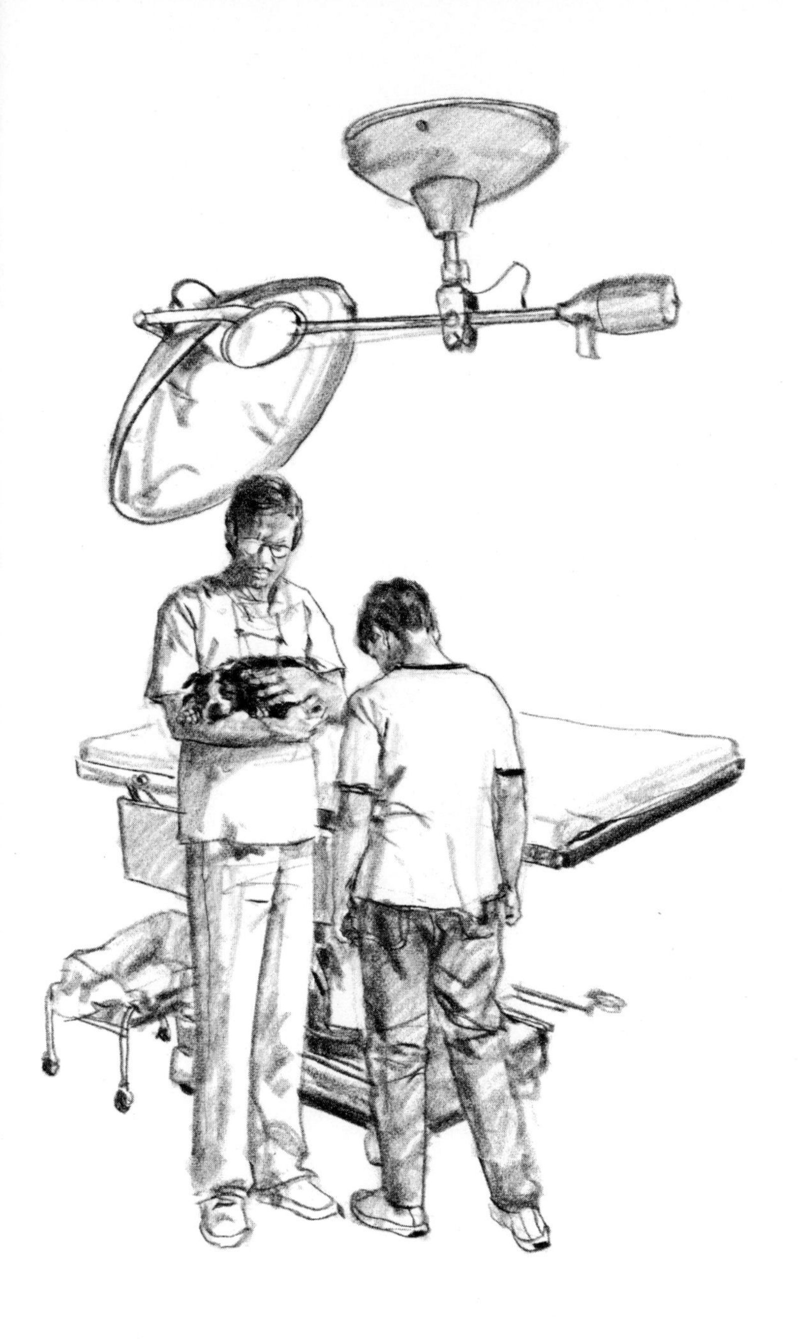

We'll keep him here for a few days. I'll phone you as soon as I think it's safe to take him home."

Mr. Zamora thanked him and started for the parking lot with Marc and Kiki trailing after him. "How did you get down here?" he asked Marc.

"My bike." said Marc.

"Put it in the back of the truck," said Mr. Zamora. "We'll give you a lift up the hill."

Marc was grateful. His knees felt too weak and wobbly to get him up that canyon road.

SHEEPHERDER'S BEANS

Friday, February fifth, the day of the camp-out, was warm. At noon Marc and Gonny sat on a shady bench in the school yard, eating their lunch. Kiki came running up to them, looking as though he would burst with excitement.

"Marc," he cried, "how goes your *mamá* sewing the new zipper on the sleeping bag? Please, Marc, I beg you to call her and say the zipper is not necessary. Am I a baby that I need a zipper on my sleeping bag?"

"It's my bag, and you're just borrowing it," Marc told him. "The zipper was broken, and when my mom does something she does it right."

He offered Kiki half a sandwich, but Kiki backed off. "Would choke me," he protested. "I have much on the mind. I worry does your *mamá* finish the zipper, I worry does Mr. Zamora get my things to Mr. Brenner's in time, and always I worry for fear I get left behind."

"I'm going too, you know," Marc reminded him. "And good old Gonny is going to help us."

Gonny made a gagging sound. "Good old Gonny needs his head examined," he said. "No one in his right mind would leave his comfortable bed at home to go out and sleep on a pile of rocks."

"They might go off and leave us," Kiki insisted.

"Look," said Marc, "Mr. Zamora promised to pick up our camping equipment and deliver everything to Mr. Brenner's. Right? And Mr. Zamora is a man of his word, right? And no matter how rattled you get, Mr. Brenner is not going to take off without us."

Still Kiki was not entirely satisfied. "I hope he doesn't forget the pot of beans," he said.

"No one's bringing any pot of beans," Marc said impatiently.

"Mr. Zamora brings them," said Kiki. "Once he herds the sheeps in a place called Nevada. There he makes the sheeps herder's beans in a big iron pot. He loans me the pot, and last night we soak the beans with soda, so they be ready to cook at our camp-out. Mr. Zamora teach me to cook the beans. I will not fail."

"I hate to break this bad news to you, Kiki," said Marc, "but Mr. Brenner is not about to take a pot of sloppy uncooked beans to the mountains. That's final."

"Was final at first," Kiki agreed. "But after I phone him only four times to explain, he says please to bring the beans and to forget the telephoning. He was very polite."

"I'll bet," said Gonny. "It's guys like you who make men like Mr. Brenner swear off good deeds for life."

Kiki didn't get the point. He looked across the playground and, spying someone he knew, yelled, "Hey, Frederico, wait a minute. I have a question."

"The nervous wreck," said Gonny, as Kiki ran off.

"I've never seen a kid like him," Marc agreed.

"And you never will," said Gonny.

After school they rode the three blocks to Mr. Brenner's house. The front yard was littered with cub scouts, piles of camping equipment, and uneasy parents, who seemed to feel they had to stand around until the show got on the road.

Kiki was there, bent under the weight of his sleeping bag, as he moved it from one spot to another. When he saw Marc and Gonny, he dropped his burden and ran to meet them.

"Leave the bicycles in the garage," he directed with authority, motioning them on down the driveway. "Then you can help pack the station wagon."

Gonny's eyebrows shot up. "You giving the orders around here now?" he asked.

Kiki waved him on. "Everybody has to help Mr. Brenner," he said with dignity. "One *papá* who promises to go on the camp-out gets the car broke down and cannot go. The other *papá* brings the car,

but he can squeeze in only six cubs. Mr. Brenner's station wagon must take all the rest. I fear I will get left behind."

"No such luck," said Gonny.

Kiki, though, was spared the insult, for he had run off to speak to Mr. Brenner.

"We could load thirty elephants and twenty camels with half the fuss," Gonny said.

"After this," said Marc, "every gripe costs you a nickel. What we need around here is less talk and more action."

The safari finally got under way at four forty-two. The luggage rack on top of Mr. Brenner's station wagon was piled high with bedrolls as they headed for Camp Pierce.

They drove the coast highway. Forty miles past Malibu they took the right-hand turn to Yerba Canyon, which led to the locked gate guarding the entrance to Camp Pierce.

Kiki sat on the very back seat of the station wagon, squeezed in beside Marc and Gonny. He craned his neck to get a better look at the sparsely wooded hills that led into the mountains.

"The sign on the gate said *private*," he observed. "That means we own the *rancho*?"

"Not quite," said Marc. "Mr. Pierce owns it. He's going to build a home up here someday, but in the meantime we get to use it."

"That's good," said Kiki. "Not as good as if we own it, but better than nothing." He leaned over to check on the black iron pot that he was using for a footrest. "I worry about the beans," he confided. "Maybe Mr. Brenner did wrong to make me pour off the water before we started."

Marc gave him an impatient shove with his elbow. "Don't be silly. Who wants water spilled all over everything? You can add water before you cook them."

"All I know," said Kiki solemnly, "they got to be the best beans any cub ever tasted."

"Beans are beans," said Marc. "Forget it."

However, the moment Mr. Brenner crossed the last culvert and parked in the clearing beneath a big oak tree, Kiki scrambled past Marc and reached for his precious pot. He set it off to one side behind the protection of a big root, not forgetting to put a rock on the top to keep the three-legged pot from overturning in the event an earthquake decided to strike before the cooking fire was ready.

Afterward he was all over the place. He tore up the hillside helping collect wood for the campfire, he washed his mess kit, and he moved his sleeping bag four times before he was sure he wouldn't be run over by a buffalo stampede during the night.

"Now I know what they mean about a little learning being a dangerous thing," Gonny told Marc. "Did you hear Kiki con Mr. Brenner into letting him make a special fire for his beans? We're going to feast on beans tomorrow whether we like them or not."

"What's one campfire more or less?" Marc said. "If he wants to bring in the wood, who's to object? Those beans are some kind of a status deal to him. Have you noticed how he struts in front of Erv Tatum? He even has the gall to leave the handle of his slingshot sticking up out of his hip pocket."

"I'm about to move over on Erv's side," said Gonny. "That Kiki is worse than a swarm of bees. He's all over the place. He's so helpful he's wrecking the whole camp."

Marc nodded. "Even Mr. Brenner knows he's here,"

he agreed. "Used to be when you said the name Kiki, he would ask, Kiki who? But not anymore. He knows!"

"Don't we all?" said Gonny.

Kiki made a big production of the special fire for the beans. After supper when the other boys were gathered around the campfire pit, he got busy piling brush over his big black pot.

"That's no way to cook beans," Marc told him. "You're supposed to let the fire die down, and then set the pot in the red-hot coals with a few coals on the top. Any scout knows that much."

Kiki tried to be patient. "The sheeps herder's way is best," he said with unshaken confidence. "Mr. Zamora tells me over and over just what to do. With the beans is the soda, the onions, and the bits of ham. Please, if you don't talk so much, maybe you learn something."

Gonny beckoned to Marc. "After all, they're his beans," he said.

There was one slight emergency. The beans were in place with the black pot all but lost under a pile of brush; Kiki had succeeded in lighting one crackling branch when he began to yell and beat at the flame with a wet gunnysack that covered the cartons of milk.

"Stop the fire," he begged. "I forgot to put in the water."

Several boys extinguished the fire and refilled the pot with water, and with much labor, Kiki got started again. When the fire was leaping wildly around the black pot, Marc turned away.

"Sheepherders or no sheepherders," he told Gonny, "it doesn't stand to reason that a pot can survive in that inferno, much less a bunch of beans."

"Oh, well," said Gonny, "tomorrow after we get these kids up to Lookout Point and back, maybe a little melted iron pot will taste pretty good."

Marc kept a watchful eye on Kiki's fire as he settled around the big campfire with the other boys. In fact, he moved in closer and closer with the other kids, for a chilly breeze was blowing down the canyon. By bedtime Marc was well toasted on the front side and half frozen on the back side.

There was great activity as the cubs settled in their sleeping bags for the night. Each one of them seemed to have a rock piercing a tender part of his anatomy and so kept moving his bag from one spot to the other until overcome by cold and exhaustion.

Marc's duty was to make a bed check at eleven o'clock.

"That's crazy," Gonny protested, when Marc asked to borrow his big flashlight. "Who's getting out of a warm sleeping bag to wander around in the cold?"

"Some of the kids have to get up at night, same as at home," said Marc. "Nothing to it. I just go around and count the twelve heads, and that's it."

"Who's going to wake you up?" Gonny asked. "Don't look at me. Once in the hay I sleep like a log."

"Mr. Brenner loaned me his traveling clock," said Marc. "He set the alarm for eleven on the nose."

Gonny took off his boots, pulled a green knit cap down over his ears, and crawled into his sleeping bag. "Happy head hunting, pal," he said.

Marc retired into his dad's sleeping bag. It had an air mattress, so he was luxuriously protected from the bumps and rocks. Kiki was using his own bag. Marc wasted no time getting to sleep, but it seemed that he barely had closed his eyes when the shrill little alarm buzzed under his ear. He lifted his head, trying to get rid of the sound, and woke up enough to know that he hadn't the slightest intention of attending to any bed check. After all, what kid was stupid enough to wander off in the dark and fall into a cold creek when he could stay in his nice cozy sleeping bag?

Despite himself, he wriggled out of his bag with a groan and pulled on his boots. He tucked the laces inside, so he wouldn't trip on them. It wouldn't take more than a minute or so to check those twelve heads, he kept telling himself.

The broad beam of the flashlight picked out the twelve sleeping bags, but there were only eleven heads. One sleeping bag was empty. Marc glanced in the direction of the washroom, expecting to see the beam of another flashlight, but all was darkness. He clumped down the path, wondering what boy had gone so far at this time of night. Boy, was it ever cold!

He searched the washroom and the showers, but no one was there. Then he hurried back up the path, pursued by dark shadows, and counted the sleeping heads again. Eleven heads, not counting Gonny, Mr. Brenner, and the father who was his assistant.

Where was that other kid? Marc gritted his teeth to keep them steady as he made a more careful check. Still only eleven heads. This time he recognized the empty sleeping bag as his own. It was Kiki who was missing. Marc hurried over to the spot where the black pot sat in a ring of ashes, but Kiki was not there.

Close to panic, Marc hurried to Gonny. He shook him and peeled back the trap and covers until Gonny's nose was exposed to the chill night air.

"Gonny, I need your help," Marc told him in a hoarse whisper. "Kiki is missing."

"Good," muttered Gonny. "Now we can relax."

Marc shook him harder. "Gonny! This is serious. I'm responsible for these kids. Come on, we've got to find Kiki."

He all but dragged Gonny from his nice warm cocoon. This time Gonny went around shining the light on the various heads.

"Let's start yelling," he proposed. "That should bring him in."

"You crazy!" protested Marc. "You want to have Mr. Brenner on our tail? Kiki's got to be around here somewhere."

"We're always trying to ditch him," grumbled Gonny. "Why should we look for him now?"

Marc went to Kiki's sleeping bag. He felt inside to see if it was still warm, trying to figure how long Kiki had been gone. His cold hands met a warm wetness.

"Oh, my gosh," he exclaimed to Gonny. "He wet the bed."

"That explains everything," said Gonny. "He's jumped in the creek to drown himself."

Marc took the light from Gonny and made another determined inspection of the sleeping bags. The one that bore the head of Erv Tatum looked especially bulky. Marc bent low over Erv and felt deep down beside him. Sure enough, there was another head burrowed under the covers. Marc's light shone on Kiki's black hair.

"Here he is," Marc told Gonny. "He's crawled in with Erv. They're both sound asleep."

Gonny took a look. "He sure found a way to get even with Erv," he said. "Erv will die with his boots on when he finds he's been cuddling up to Kiki."

"We've got to get Kiki out of there," Marc said. "If this ever gets around, he's ruined for life."

"Well, he's not going to get in my bed." said Gonny.

"He's not going to get in my bed," Marc agreed.

"We sound like the bears and Goldilocks," said Gonny. "Why don't we just drag him out in the morning before Erv wakes up?"

Marc jerked the wet blanket from Kiki's sleeping

bag. "Come on," he urged. "Let's spread this on one of those mesquite bushes, so it can dry out. After all, we've got another night out here."

Hastily they took the blanket to one side and spread it over a growth of mesquite, anchoring it on the husky thorns.

"That ought to do it," said Marc, sucking a place on his thumb where a thorn had caught him.

Gonny was too disgusted to speak. He hurried back to his warm sleeping bag and paused only long enough to tug off his boots before he crawled inside. Marc was so cold and sleepy by then that he could quite understand how Kiki, in his emergency, had crawled into the first dry sleeping bag he found.

The next morning Marc and Gonny pulled Kiki out into the brisk morning air while Erv was still asleep. Kiki had dried off, and he actually didn't seem to know why or when he had wandered in the night.

"How you think I got in that bag with Erv?" he asked.

"You were looking for a dry spot," said Marc. "Your blanket is over on that mesquite drying out."

Kiki was indignant. "I don' do such a thing," he said positively. "I stop that baby stuff long ago."

Marc looked questioningly at Gonny, as if to ask him what they should do.

"It's like bad breath," said Gonny. "Nobody's ever going to admit he has it."

Kiki was watching them with the look of a person who was trying to awaken from a bad dream.

"So we forget it," said Marc. "Neither of us will mention it to anyone."

"Okay," Gonny agreed. "But it seems a shame not to kid Erv about his bedmate."

On the other hand, the matter of the beans was nothing anyone could hide. Kiki had made such a big production number of the bean ceremony the night before that all the kids gathered around the pot the first thing. They wanted to see the delicious sheepherder's beans that would melt in their mouths and bring recognition to the new cub scout who was such a stickler for perfection.

Kiki dusted off the film of white ashes that covered the top of the pot. He lifted off the lid with a stick. The lid was so heavy that it fell to one side, and everyone got a good look. At first glance the pot seemed empty. Then closer inspection revealed dozens of little pellets, no larger than BB shot, at the bottom of the pot, each one resting in its own tiny crater.

Kiki looked stricken, as if he couldn't believe what he saw. He knew that his attempt was raw disaster, but he couldn't figure what had happened. "I did everything like Mr. Zamora say," he cried. "But something goes wrong."

He got no argument. Such a terrible disgrace was too much for any one cub to be called on to face. The other kids stared at the ruined pot and the cremated beans. Quietly they turned away, one by one, and tried to melt into the landscape. They behaved as one does at the funeral of a pet dog or cat that has suffered a disappointing end.

As for Kiki, if the pot had been large enough, he would have crawled in on the bed of horror and pulled the top over him. He was forever disgraced.

SIX POINT FIVE

Monday afternoon, as Marc and Gonny were leaving the school grounds, Kiki hailed them. "Hey, you," he called, "How about a ride to the foot of the hill? I go to stay with my friend, Mr. Zamora."

"Your Chicano sure bounces back in a hurry," Gonny told Marc with a grin. "Wait until you hear how he set up the cub camp at Pierce last Friday. To hear him tell it, he did every single chore just right for two whole days. He's broadcast to everyone the good news that he's to receive his bobcat badge Friday. He's getting so cocky he needs spurs."

"He's not so bad," Marc said. "It's just that I get sick and tired of having everyone call him my Chicano."

"It just slipped out," said Gonny.

The trouble was, the phrase always kept slipping out. When any of the kids saw Marc hurrying somewhere, they would point up or down, east or west, and yell, "Your little Chicano went thataway."

Apparently they were hard up for humor. And Gonny was no help at all. He listened to the teasing, his mocking eyes on Marc. Was he not the one who had warned Marc to stay clear of Kiki? Still, Marc was determined not to give Gonny or any of the other kids the satisfaction of turning him against Kiki. Not in the open anyway. But in his own heart he was uneasy. He doubted the association was doing Kiki any good. Having an older boy to lean on made him more demanding than ever. No matter what bothered him, he came straight to Marc with his problem, sure that his important friend would come up with the right answer.

Now here he was again, showing his white teeth in an eager smile. "You give me the ride, yes?" he asked Marc.

All the kids around heard him. "Sure, Marc," yelled Erv Tatum, "give your little Chicano a ride. Give him two rides."

Very funny, Marc thought, hustling Kiki onto his bicycle. He even managed a smile as they took off.

Gonny rode along beside them, extra cheerful. "You can wipe that smile off your face now," he called to Marc. "No one around but us *amigos*."

Kiki chimed in happily, "Sure, nobody here but friends. I guess maybe this is the happiest day of my life."

That was another irritating thing about Kiki. He was always knee-deep in the happiest day of his life. All this happiness talk made Marc uneasy. It was sort of an extra burden and made him feel he always should be shoveling happiness at the guy.

Gonny nodded toward the newspaper-wrapped parcel that Kiki carried, thrust between his shirt and the top of his pants. "What you got there?" he asked.

"My other shirt," said Kiki. "I stay for a week or more with my friend, Mr. Zamora."

"What's the idea?" Gonny asked.

"My sister, Delores, got the little red bumps," said Kiki. "Maybe is the chicken pox. Mr. Zamora keeps me till all is clear."

Gonny nodded as though he had known all along what to expect. "Fair enough," he said cheerfully. "Marc gives you a ride, and you give him chicken pox."

"Sure," said Kiki, as cocky as ever. "For me he does the favors. I am his Chicano."

The anger Marc had kept bottled up inside him boiled over. He braked the bicycle so suddenly that Kiki went halfway over the handlebars before he could regain his balance. "Get off and stay off," Marc ordered. "You are not my Chicano. I've never had chicken pox, and I don't need it now."

Kiki moved off a step or two and stared at him, half smiling to cover his bewilderment. Apparently something was going on that he did not understand.

"You make joke?" he asked.

"No joke," Marc said shortly. "Just stay away from me, you understand?"

Kiki shook his head. *"No comprendo,"* he said.

Marc turned on Gonny, trying to vent his rage on someone his own size. "This is where you take over," he said. "From here on, Kiki is all yours."

Gonny's look of amusement changed to one of startled indignation. But he could see that Marc meant business. He also knew that Marc's bicycle was faster and lighter than his own and that Marc was in no mood to listen to flimsy excuses.

Reluctantly Gonny stopped and motioned for Kiki to perch on the crossbar of his bike. "Don't get any ideas," he warned his passenger. "This is a temporary arrangement. I'm not a soft touch like what's his name over there."

When Gonny stopped at the foot of the hill, Kiki hopped off in a hurry. "Thanks for the ride," he said. "I go to tell Mr Zamora that Friday I get my badge. He will be very proud of me." He started off, but paused to stand very straight as he gave the cub-scout salute. "See you tomorrow," he called in farewell.

Not if I can help it, Marc decided. He ignored Kiki and allowed Gonny to return the salute. This was the time to polish off that Chicano business once and for all. Kiki was as persistent as a stray pup that follows a guy home from school. He was a nuisance and an embarrassment, yet Marc was not ready to get rough with him in front of Gonny.

The next morning Marc was awakened by a spooky rumbling sound. For one dream-sodden second he thought he was shaking the stuffing out of that little pest Kiki. Then he realized that he was the one that was getting the shaking. He was in his own room. Dim daylight shone through the open slats of the Venetian blinds, and the sweet smell of pittosporum blossoms filled the air. The rumbling increased to a roar. Could the sonar blast of a jet aircraft be jarring the house? Suddenly his bed did a double roll, and he found himself on the floor. His cry of protest was lost in the creaking and grinding of the house as it shook and vibrated.

A shattering blast of broken glass exploded in the

hallway. Crashes and thuds came from inside and outside the house. Suddenly Marc realized what was happening. "Earthquake!" he shouted.

He tripped on the bedcovers as he lurched toward the door, ran down the hallway, and barged into his parents' room. Mrs. Conley was trying to get her arms into the sleeves on her pink robe, while Mr. Conley urged her to the open doorway that led to the bathroom.

"Stand there," he said. "It's safer."

He put a firm hand on Marc's shoulder and moved him to the other doorway. Marc braced himself. The Venetian blinds clattered, the bedside lamp tottered. Something slid from the dresser top and crashed to the floor. Marc's teeth were chattering, his stomach was a knot, and his heart thudded so hard he could scarcely breathe.

The quake was shaking his house the way Tarzan shook Butch when they were fighting. "Don't panic," he kept telling himself. "Don't panic." He had been in quakes before, but whoever heard of one so savage that it went on and on forever?

He was clinging to his dad with both hands before

the awful vibrations seemed to ease off a little. Slowly he took a quivering breath as he began to get a welcome back-to-earth feeling. His father crossed to the big window that overlooked the San Fernando Valley, and Marc stayed close at his side. Clouds of brownish smoke hid the sunrise and dimmed the flicker of erupting fires.

"What are those bursts of blue light down there?" Marc whispered.

"Electrical explosions and transformers going out," said his father.

"What are all those water spouts?" he asked.

"They're broken water mains."

"Is it over?" Marc said, still whispering as though he feared he might set off a fresh upheaval. "Oh, oh! There goes another one."

His father staggered as he turned away from the window and reached for his trousers. "That's an aftershock," he said. "We'll get plenty of those."

"That first one was a real stinker," said Marc, wondering what was making him feel so strange.

"Must have registered a six point four or five on

the Richter Scale," his father agreed. "Could have been a point six."

Marc's strange inner disturbance erupted in a volcanic surge that sent him rushing past his mother to the bathroom. He heaved up a hot mess of sourish swill and shuddered time and again before he recovered enough to flush the toilet. He took the pink plastic glass from its holder over the washbasin intending to rinse out his mouth. When he turned on the cold-water faucet, however, there was a gurgling, a hollow sucking sound, and no water. Then the room began to sway.

"Just another aftershock," he told himself, as he hung on to the washbasin. "Nothing but a little old aftershock. We'll have plenty of those."

Next he tried the hot-water tap. Still no water. "Guess we've got a broken waterline of our own," he called to his father. "No water."

"Turn it off," said Mr. Conley. "I'm going outside to turn off the gas."

Marc saw that his mother was dabbing at her mouth with a washcloth. "What happened?" he asked.

His mother shook her head, as though it was nothing to worry about. "Bit my lip," she said. "I'm going to put ice on it."

Mr. Conley started to hurry down the hallway but he turned back for a moment. "We've lost the antique mirror," he announced. "It's all over the floor. Marc,

watch it as you go through here, or you'll get glass in your feet."

"I already did," said Marc. "I feel a sliver in my toe."

"Well, get it out," said his father. "And put some clothes on. We'll need a good helper around here."

When Marc returned to his room, he saw that his bed had been moved over against the far wall. His alarm clock had smashed to the floor and stopped running at forty-two seconds past six o'clock. He stepped over scattered books and papers to straighten the calendar that hung over his desk. With shaking hands he removed the cap from a red felt-tipped pen and made an uneven circle around the date, Tuesday, February the ninth.

"Boy, I'll never forget this day," he told himself with a shudder. "Never!"

THE DOVECOTE

"Marc," his mother called from the hallway. "Bring a carton from the garage. We've got to clean up this glass."

"Just a minute," said Marc. "First I've got to find my other shoe."

As he went out the back door, he heard the sirens of ambulances, police cars, and fire engines wailing down on the boulevard. He found his father with a big Stillson wrench in his hand, listening to the news on the car radio.

"The north end of the valley was the hardest hit," he told Marc. "And there's no school today."

No school? It didn't seem possible. Marc moved in beside his father and listened to the radio report: two big hospitals had fallen apart, overpasses had collapsed and were blocking the freeways, the Van Norman Reservoir, holding three to four billion gallons of water, had been damaged, and the sixty thousand residents who lived below it were ordered from their homes.

"Where will all those people go?" Marc asked.

"They'll have to stay with friends or relatives or sleep in evacuation centers that will be set up in the schools," said Mr. Conley.

"Will they use my school?" Marc asked.

"Possibly, if it's safe," said his father.

Suddenly Marc heard a new wailing sound, "Marc! Marc!" Then there came running footsteps pounding up the driveway. Gonny was waving his arms as he ran. "It's Kiki," he cried. "He was sleeping in the room under the dovecote. The whole thing collapsed."

Marc couldn't believe any harm would come to Kiki. "Maybe be got out," he said.

"No, no," cried Gonny. "He's buried under all that stuff. Mr. Zamora and my father are digging like crazy, but they need help."

Mr. Conley didn't stop to ask questions. He put the garden mattock and a shovel in the car and started the motor. Throwing open the far door for Gonny, he said, "Hop in."

He leaned out the window to speak to Marc. "Tell your mother not to worry. I turned off the gas. I'll be back as soon as possible." He started backing down the driveway. "Phone the fire department and the police department," he added. "Get them up here. Tell them it's an emergency."

"Yes, sir," said Marc.

Mrs. Conley, hugging her pink robe around her, met Marc in the kitchen. The cupboard doors had swung open, and canned goods, kitchen utensils, and broken china and glassware littered the floor.

"Where's your dad going?" she asked.

"To Mr. Zamora's," Marc told her. "The dovecote caved in on Kiki, and I've got to get the police and the fire department."

He ran to the telephone. The two emergency numbers were written right there on the front of the telephone book. He dialed the police first. All he got in return was a busy signal. He tried the fire department number, and still he could get nothing but a busy signal.

"Should I ride my bike down to the service station on the boulevard and see if their phone is working?" he asked.

"No," said his mother. "Let your dad decide what to do."

That reminded Marc of his message. "He says you're not to worry," he told her. "He turned off the gas."

"I'm not to worry," said his mother, with such a strange look that Marc thought she was not going to let him go up the hill. Just then a strong aftershock rattled the windows, and his mother clung to the sink with both hands. When the last quiver had melted away, she glanced around the messy kitchen with the critical look of a stranger who was just passing through.

"I've got to tell Dad I can't get anyone," Marc said. "I've got to ask him what to do."

His mother nodded mutely and waved him on his way.

"Don't worry," Marc called to her, as he bolted out the back door. "We'll clean up that mess when we get back."

The house on the hill looked the same as usual from the front. He could see no added damage as he went up the driveway. A scattering of oranges lay in a circle under the two orange trees that grew near the back door, and his father's car was parked beside Mr. Zamora's pickup truck.

Tarzan and Butch came tearing around a corner of the house to greet him with their usual barking. But their welcome was hasty and mechanical, as though they merely were attending to their duty while more important matters held their attention.

Marc followed them to the far side of the house, where all the chopping and thumping was going on. The guest room and bath lay in ruin. The tile roofing was scattered all around, and the big dovecote that had perched so nicely on the roof now lay in the center of the disaster as lopsided as a candle on a stale birthday cake.

The men were working carefully with pick and shovel to clear a way through the rubble. Even Gonny was loading chunks of wire and stucco in a metal wheelbarrow.

Marc approached his father timidly. Mr. Conley straightened up and stared at him, his face glistening with sweat. "Where are the police? Where are the firemen?" he asked impatiently. "We need them."

Marc shook his head, full of apology. "I couldn't get anything but a busy signal," he said.

"I'll get help," said Mr. Conley grimly. He handed the mattock to Marc and turned to Mr. Zamora. "You'd better take a rest," he cautioned.

Mr. Zamora breathed deeply. His face was red, and his wispy white hair was plastered to his forehead with sweat. "We've got to dig," he said. "We've got to get to the boy."

Mr. Conley hurried to his car, and Marc tried to swing the mattock into the barrier of stucco, chicken

wire, and plaster as his father had been doing. The broad cutter edge of the mattock jolted him from head to toe every time it hit anything solid. He turned the mattock over to work with the slender pick end, which was a little easier to manage. But soon his arms felt numb from his wrists to his shoulders.

Tarzan and Butch tried to help. They dug furiously at the rubble and kept getting in the way.

"You'd better tie up the dogs," Mr. Zamora told Marc. "You'll find rope in the garage."

Marc got the rope, but when he returned he found that the dogs had gone around to the far side of the dovecote. Butch had wormed his way through the maze of crumpled wire and stucco. There he sniffed and barked at a slit of a window. Tarzan tried to join him, but he was too big for such close quarters.

Butch paused in his barking for a moment, and Marc heard sounds as faint as the mewing of a lost kitten.

"Kiki," he shouted.

"Help me," came the weak response from under the dovecote.

Marc got down on his hands and knees and crawled over the litter of broken stucco and plaster toward Butch. The space between the fallen dovecote and the ground narrowed. Soon he was hugging the ground. Then he reached a tighter spot, where he had to lie flat on his stomach. He eased himself along by digging in the dirt with his elbows and knees.

Slowly, slowly he inched along until he could see

the opening that once had been a window. Now it was squashed down until there was only a ten-inch space left. Marc wormed his way closer and tried to peer inside, but his sweat blinded him. He managed to get his left hand up to wipe his face and looked again. He could see a sturdy wooden bed, which was all but buried under the fallen ceiling. Bedcovers hung over the side.

"Kiki, you in there?" he called.

"I think," came Kiki's muffled voice, no more than a raspy whisper.

Marc raised up on his elbows. "Hey, Gonny," he yelled excitedly. "Kiki is here. Right here."

"We know," Gonny yelled back.

Marc peered in at the dark interior. "I can't see you," he told Kiki. "You under the covers?"

"Under the bed," said Kiki in a faraway voice.

"Hear the men digging?" Marc said, trying to encourage him. "We're going to get you out of there. Can you wriggle over here? Maybe we can squeeze you out through this opening."

"I cannot move," Kiki said.

"You can try," Marc urged. "Give me your hand. I'll help you."

Slowly a groping hand reached out of the shadows. Marc felt Kiki's cold gritty fingers close convulsively around his own.

"Do not leave me," Kiki begged. "Please not to leave me."

"I won't," Marc promised. "I'll stay right here."

Butch had managed to work his way out to the open, and now he joined Tarzan in barking a wel-

come as Mr. Conley's car returned. Soon there was renewed activity with picks and shovels, crowbars, and mattocks.

"Good," said Kiki. "Now maybe they get me out of here."

"They're really pouring it on," Marc agreed.

"Teacher say when comes the quake is safest in the open field," said Kiki. "I think is best to be horse or burro."

"You want to end up as a can of cat chow?" Marc asked.

"Ah, no," protested Kiki. "Is bad enough to be sardine under this bed."

He coughed, and his hand tensed, then went limp.

"Don't talk," Marc urged. "You all right?"

There was no answer, no slightest response.

"Kiki!" Marc cried in alarm.

Then Kiki spoke, the words spaced carefully. "I

think best you leave me," he said. "The diggers get close. Is better you show them where to find me."

"I promised not to leave you," Marc reminded him.

Kiki coughed gently and waited to get his breath. "I thought I was dead," he explained. "Now is different. I not afraid."

Marc squeezed his hand reassuringly. "I won't go far," he said. "I'll get over on the other side and see what I can do."

He tried to back out, but got tangled in a mass of the tough bougainvillaea vine which had stickers on it that felt as sharp as the point of a red-hot ice pick.

A hand gripped his left ankle. "Hey, Marc," Gonny called, "you're going the wrong way. Let me have your other foot and I'll pull you out of there."

Marc allowed himself to be dragged on his stomach over the messy rubble. Gonny helped him to his feet.

"Is Kiki hurt bad?" he asked.

"Who knows?" said Marc, brushing past him. "First we get him out of there. Then we ask the questions."

As he picked his way around the debris of the fallen dovecote, he heard a triumphant shout. When he reached the men working around the excavation, he saw that his father was down in the cramped space they had cleared. He was straining at one end of a heavy iron bar that lifted the lower end of Kiki's bed.

"Quick, Marc," he called. "Get down here. Pull the boy clear."

Gingerly Marc crawled over the slabs of stucco and wire and lowered himself down in the hole beside his father. Kiki lay there with his eyes tightly shut, nothing visible except his head and arms. He was so heavily powdered with plaster that he looked like a fallen statue. Marc caught hold of Kiki under the arms and tugged gently until he was pulled free and could be lifted in Marc's arms. Strong hands reached down and hauled the two of them from the dusty shadows to the bright sunlight.

At last Kiki dared open his eyes. He blinked at the strong light and tried to wriggle free. "Put me down," he begged Marc. "I wish to see is all of me here."

Marc eased him to the ground. Kiki held onto him as he tried his weight on first one foot and then the other. He blew fiercely from his nostrils, then took a cautious deep breath. A smile broke through the film of powdery plaster. He turned his back on Marc and leaned against him as though he were a post put there for his convenience. He looked from one to the other of his rescuers whose broad smiles matched his own.

"Thank you," he told them. "You are my good friends." He turned to Marc. "Please, you tell them. From me it sounds not so good, but I want them to know they don' save just a boy, they save a bobcat."

"What he means," Marc explained to the men, "is that he's now a cub scout."

Gonny caught Kiki's arm and raised it high in the manner of a referee at a boxing match. "The winner!" he cried.

Mr. Zamora led the cheering. Marc grinned as he saw Kiki's wriggle of delight. Mr. Conley hurried to gather up his digging implements.

"Sorry to break up this fine gathering," he said, "but Marc and I are needed at home." He turned to Mr. Zamora. "Get the boy cleaned up, and we'll check on him later."

Mr. Zamora nodded. Kiki moved in on Marc and gave him a punch on the arm.

"We *amigos* again, yes?" he questioned.

"Amigos," Marc agreed.

And he took time out to give Kiki a sharp cub-scout salute.